Raw Family

Text and illustrations copyright © 2011 by Victoria Boutenko

www.rawfamily.com

ISBN 978-0-9704819-1-7

Library of Congress Control Number: 2011903668
Printed in Canada

Fruits I Love

Victoria Boutenko

Illustrations by
Katya Korobkina

When I see a produce stand,
I can never understand,
How can fruit of many colors,
Come from brown dirt and sand!

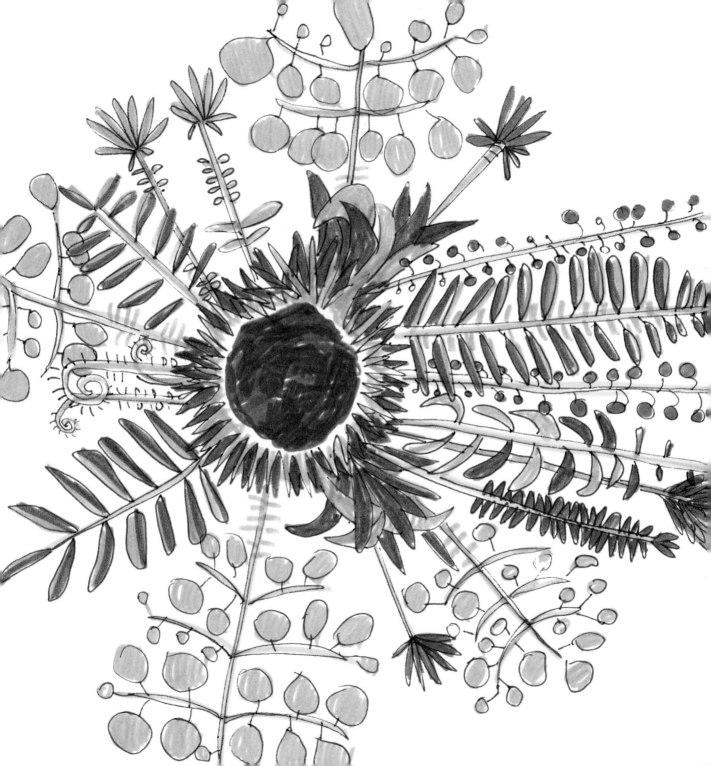

I like it yellow,
red or striped,

But most of all
I like fruit ripe!

Fruit resembles candy,
Colorful and cute,
Or maybe it is candy,
That looks and tastes like fruit?

Grapes are round like marbles,
Filled with sweetest juice.
Between red, green, or purple
Sometimes it's hard to choose.

Star fruit lifts me to the skies,
I get a star with every slice.

Cherries are so cheering,
They look like pretty earrings.
Even little fairies,
Are fond of eating cherries.

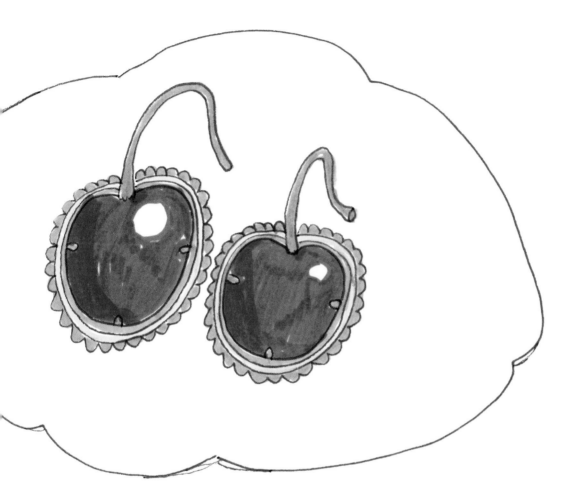

Pomegranate — jewelry box
But without any locks!
Full of sweet and juicy seeds,
They look like shiny ruby beads.

Berries too are precious!
Brightly colored treasures:
They can make incredible
Bracelets that are edible.

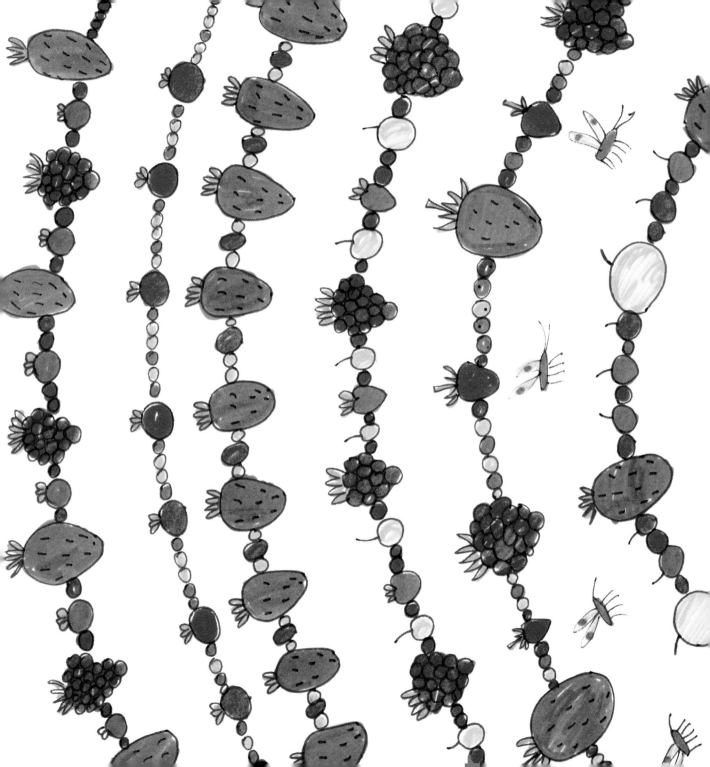

Pineapples grow on tropic farms
On bush-like, spiky mini palms.
Every fruit within the crop
Wears a little palm on top.

Sweet bananas
can convert

Any food
into dessert.

Watermelon full of juice
It is dripping on my shoes.
So tasty and exquisite,
That I'm all covered with it!

Ripe apricots are tender
And easy to divide.

Crack the pit wide open
And eat the seed inside.

I am fond of eating plums,
'Cause they don't leave any crumbs!
I can eat them in my bed,
Oops … my covers are purple instead!

Would you care for some pear?
It is sweeter than éclair.

In the summer on the beach,
I like to eat a fuzzy peach.

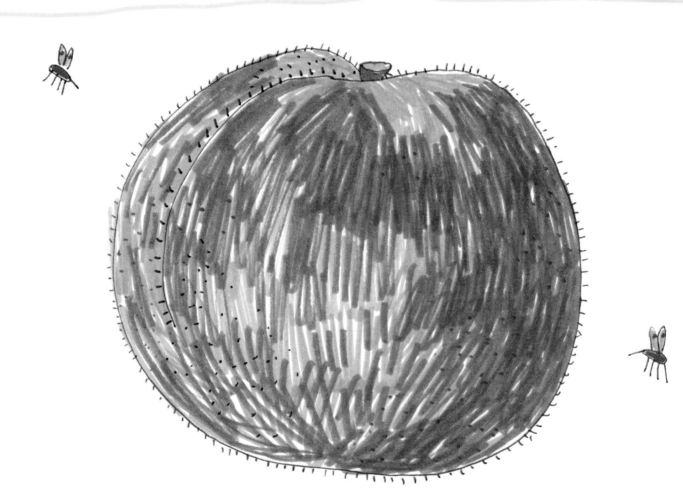

Nectarines are full of sweetness,
Eat one and become a witness!

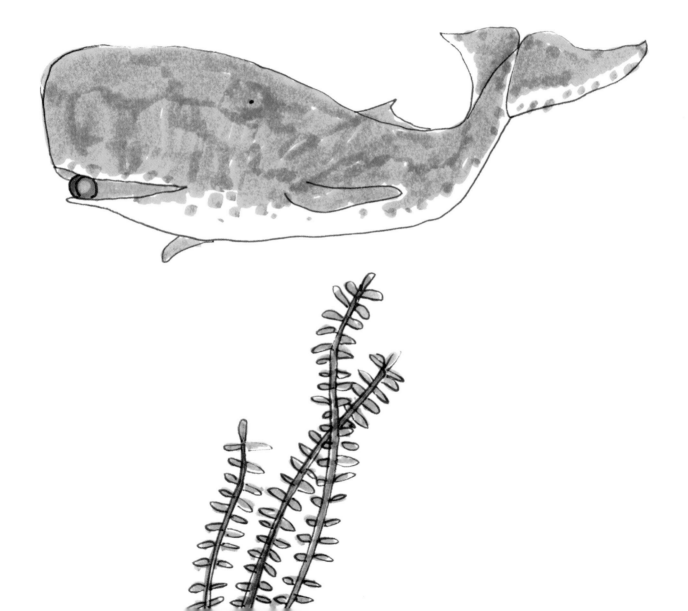

Keep an apple in your pack
For a fast and healthy snack.

Mango is a sweet surprise
Pleasant for my lips and eyes!

A slice of Mexican papaya,
Shows off the color of a fire.

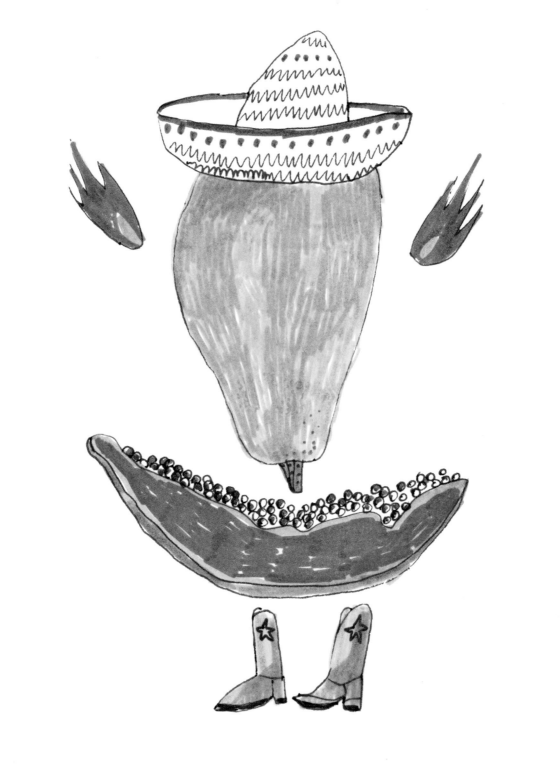

Fresh figs are magically made
With delicious marmalade.

Ripe green kiwi is quite a treat,
But golden kiwi is twice as sweet!

Orange brothers look like twins:
Tangerines and Mandarins.

I told my parents: **I Love Fruit**!
As fruit is healthy, sweet and cute.

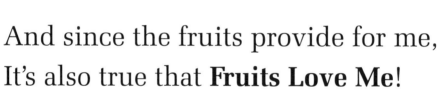

And since the fruits provide for me,
It's also true that **Fruits Love Me**!